The Boxcar Children Mysteries

THE MYSTERY AT THE DOG SHOW

created by
GERTRUDE CHANDLER WARNER

Illustrated by Charles Tang

SCHOLASTIC INC.
New York Toronto London Auckland Sydney

ISBN 0-590-46066-8

12 11 10 9 8 7 6 5 4 3 2   3 4 5 6 7 8/9

Printed in the U.S.A.   40

First Scholastic printing, July 1993

Contents

CHAPTER 1

A Dog Show in Greenfield

"Faster!" shouted six-year-old Benny Alden. "I'll race you to the bottom of the hill!" He leaned over and started pedaling his bicycle as fast as his short legs could go down the long hill at the end of Wildwood Road.

"Hey," said Jessie, Benny's older sister, who was twelve. "You have a head start." She pedaled after Benny. A moment later Benny's older brother, fourteen-year-old Henry, and his other sister, Violet, who was ten, were racing after Benny, too.

"It's a tie, it's a tie!" shouted Jessie as the four Alden children coasted to a stop at the bottom of the hill.

"No, it's not," said Benny.

"What do you mean, Benny?" asked Violet. "We all got to the bottom of the hill at exactly the same time."

Benny shook his head and pointed. "You forgot Watch. He got here before all of us!"

The four Alden children all looked at the happy, panting dog. He had come to live with them when they first became orphans and were living in an old abandoned boxcar in the woods. They'd been on their own, trying to take care of themselves. When a dog had limped into their lives with a thorn in his paw, it had seemed only right to take care of him, too. So Jessie had taken the thorn out and Benny had named the brave little dog Watch. He had been a good friend and watchdog, too, ever since.

Now the Boxcar Children no longer had to live in the boxcar in the woods. They hadn't known it then, but they had a grandfather who had been searching and searching for them. He'd found them at last and brought them all to live in his big, wonderful old house in Greenfield. And he had even had their boxcar moved to the backyard behind the house, so they could visit it whenever they wanted.

"Arf!" said Watch.

"Look at Watch." Henry laughed. "He knows he won!"

Watch ran around them in a big circle, wagging his tail so hard it looked like he was about to fall over.

"Okay, Watch," said Jessie, laughing too. She threw up her hands. "I give up. You're right, Benny. Watch is the winner!"

"Good boy, Watch," said Benny. "Hooray for you!"

"Arra-arrf!" answered Watch, making them all laugh harder.

At last Henry took a deep breath and managed to stop laughing. "Hey, we'd better be getting back home! It's almost dinnertime."

The four Alden children and Watch turned toward home. They'd been at the

Greenfield Park all afternoon. It had been a wonderful day.

They were almost home when Jessie suddenly put her brakes on and coasted to a stop.

The others stopped, too.

"What is it, Jessie?" asked Violet.

"Look. There's Dr. Scott's office. Isn't it time for Watch to have his annual shots for rabies and distemper and everything?"

"You're right," said Henry. "Let's go in and make an appointment right now."

They walked their bikes over to the side of the veterinarian's office building and parked them. But when they got to the front door, Benny said, "I'm not going in."

"Oh, Benny," said Violet. "Why not? You like Dr. Scott."

It was true. Benny did like Dr. Scott. They all did, ever since they'd helped out at the Greenfield Animal Shelter, where Dr. Scott sometimes worked.

"Yes, *I* like Dr. Scott," agreed Benny. "But *Watch* doesn't like to go to the veterinarian's office. He doesn't like to get shots! So I'll stay out here with Watch."

Henry smiled. "You're right Benny," he said. "I don't think anybody likes to get shots, even though they are for your own good. You can wait here with Watch and we'll be right back."

Henry, Jessie, and Violet went inside. Benny sat down on the steps next to Watch and put his arm around the dog.

"Don't worry," said Benny. "I'll go in with you when you have to get your shots."

Watch wagged his tail and put his paw on Benny's arm.

Inside the veterinarian's office, the receptionist looked at the three Alden children over the top of his glasses and smiled. "Hello," he said. "What can I do for you?"

"We'd like to make an appointment with Dr. Scott for our dog, Watch," explained Jessie.

"I'm sorry. Dr. Scott is away on vacation. Another veterinarian is handling her patients if there's an emergency," the receptionist told them.

"No, it isn't an emergency," said Henry. "Could we make an appointment now to see

Dr. Scott when she gets back? Our dog Watch needs his annual shots."

"Certainly," said the receptionist. He ran his finger down the page of the appointment book. "I have an appointment right after lunch the first day Dr. Scott's back in the office."

"Great," said Henry.

"Please make it in the name of Watch Alden," Violet said.

With a smile, the receptionist wrote *Watch Alden* down in the appointment book, then wrote the time and date on a card and gave it to the Aldens.

After thanking the receptionist, Henry, Jessie, and Violet went outside to join Benny and Watch. They rode quickly home to join Grandfather Alden for dinner.

As always, Mrs. McGregor, the Aldens' housekeeper, had made a wonderful dinner. And as always, Benny had seconds of everything and still had plenty of room for dessert.

"Ummm," said Benny, starting to eat the warm apple pie with ice cream that Mrs. McGregor had made for them.

Henry shook his head. "You have a *big* appetite, Benny."

"I'm still a growing boy," said Benny. "That's what Grandfather says, isn't it, Grandfather?"

Grandfather Alden chuckled. "It certainly is," he told his youngest grandchild. Then he reached in his pocket and pulled out a letter. "Before I start my dessert, I want to share some good news with you all."

"What is it, Grandfather?" asked Violet.

"This is a letter from my old friend Mrs. Annabel Teague. She and her daughter will be in town next week for the first annual Greenfield Dog Show at the Greenfield Center."

"Neat," said Jessie. Then she smiled. "I can solve the mystery of why she's coming, too!"

Grandfather's eyes twinkled. He knew his grandchildren loved mysteries and that they were very good at solving them, too. "What is the answer, Jessie?" he asked.

"She's going to be *in* the dog show," guessed Jessie.

His eyes still twinkling, Grandfather said, "Well, not exactly. *She's* not going to be in the dog show — but her golden retriever, Sunny, is!"

"Oh, Grandfather," laughed Jessie, and the others joined in, enjoying his little joke.

Then Violet asked,"What are the Teagues like, Grandfather?"

"Well, Mrs. Teague is a kind, generous person. I haven't seen her daughter, Caryn, since she was a little girl, but I remember she was a smart, active child. She's sixteen now, and it's no surprise to me that she's the one who will actually be showing Sunny in the dog show."

"How exciting," exclaimed Jessie.

"Yes it is," said Grandfather. "Caryn has had plenty of practice, it seems. Sunny has won lots and lots of prizes with Caryn showing her."

"Oh, may we go to the dog show?" asked Benny. "Please Grandfather? And see Sunny?"

"Of course, Benny. We'll all go." Grandfather paused and looked solemnly around the table. "But . . . how would you like for the Teagues and Sunny to stay with us while they're here for the show?"

"That would be great!" exclaimed Benny.

"Yes," said Jessie.

Henry and Violet agreed, too.

"Good," said Grandfather. "I'll get in touch with Annabel right away to make arrangements."

"Maybe we can help Caryn get Sunny ready for the show. We can help give Sunny a bath and brush her and take her for walks," said Violet.

"I wonder what else you have to do to get ready for a dog show," said Jessie thoughtfully. "I bet we'll learn a lot. I can hardly wait!"

"Can we enter Watch in the show?" asked Benny. "He could win lots and lots of prizes, too!"

Grandfather hid a smile. "I don't think so, Benny. You have to be a certain kind of dog."

"Watch is very brave and smart," said Benny.

"But he's not a particular breed of dog,"

said Henry. "I think only special breeds of dogs can be in a dog show."

"Yes," said Grandfather. "For this dog show, your dog must be registered with the American Kennel Club. The dog's mother and father have to be registered, too."

"Oh," said Benny. He looked at Watch, who was sitting by the dining room door. "Well, that's okay, Watch. You don't mind, do you?"

Watch tilted his head. "Arrf," he said, and they all laughed.

CHAPTER 2

Watch Makes a Friend

"Benny! Benny, where are you?" Jessie was trying to find her brother.

She looked into Violet's room. "Have you seen Benny?"

"No." Violet shook her head. "Did you ask Henry?"

"Not yet." Jessie started down the hall to Henry's room just as he came out. "Henry, have you see Benny? It's almost time for the Teagues and Sunny to get here."

"I'm ready," said Henry. "But I haven't seen Benny. Have you looked in his room?"

Jessie nodded. "Yes, but he's not there."

"Maybe he's downstairs with Mrs. McGregor. It sure smells like something great is cooking," Henry said.

"That's a good idea. Thanks." Jessie went downstairs to the kitchen.

But Benny wasn't there.

"Mmm, it smells good, Mrs. McGregor," Jessie said, taking a deep breath.

Mrs. McGregor smiled, "That it does. There's nothing that smells as good as fresh-baked bread. Or that tastes as good, either."

"I can hardly wait," said Jessie. "It smells so good, I was sure Benny would be in here."

"No, he's not. But I have an idea if you check out back by your boxcar, you might find him," suggested Mrs. McGregor.

"Thank you," Jessie said, and hurried out the back door.

Sure enough, Benny was in front of the boxcar. He had filled an old tin washtub full of soapy water, and he and Watch were covered in water and suds.

"Benny! What are you doing?" Jessie called.

"Giving Watch a bath so when he meets Sunny, he'll be nice and clean," gasped Benny, trying to hold on to the squirming dog. Watch thought having a bath was great fun. He was splashing in the water and wriggling all around.

"Oops," said Benny, waving his arms and trying to keep his balance as Watch bumped into his legs. He tripped and fell into the washtub with Watch.

Jessie started to laugh as soap and water flew everywhere. Benny stuck his head out of the water and wiped his face. He grinned. "I guess I'll be clean, too," he said.

"I guess you will. Here, let me help you," said Jessie. She gave Benny a hand out of the washtub. Then the two of them caught Watch and soaped him all over and rinsed him gently with the hose.

"I remembered to bring a towel," said Benny proudly. He went over to the boxcar and picked up the towel he had left on the tree stump that was the boxcar's front step. Together Benny and Jessie dried off Watch.

"Watch is beautiful," declared Benny.

"He does look good," agreed Jessie. "Now, we must hurry and get ready. The Teagues and Sunny will be here any minute!"

Jessie and Benny rushed back to the house to change into clean, dry clothes. As Benny went up the back stairs into the kitchen, he looked over his shoulder.

"Don't you want to come in, Watch?" he asked.

Watch stayed where he was at the foot of the back steps.

"Okay, you can stay outside," said Benny. "But be good, now. And don't get dirty!"

The front doorbell rang just as Benny and Jessie finished getting ready. They raced down the stairs as Grandfather Alden opened the front door. Henry and Violet were there already.

In the doorway was a small woman with blue eyes and red-gold hair twisted back into a soft bun. She was wearing khaki slacks, a plaid shirt, and a blue cardigan sweater. She stepped briskly over the threshold and gave their grandfather a big hug. "James Henry

Alden," she said. "It has been a long, long time."

"Much too long, Annabel Teague," agreed Grandfather Alden, smiling.

In a moment, two more figures appeared in the doorway.

"This is my daughter, Caryn," said Mrs. Teague. "And of course, Sunny."

A tall graceful girl, who looked about sixteen, followed Mrs. Teague into the house. She had hair the same red-gold color as her mother's, but her eyes were brown instead of blue, and she wore her hair pulled back in a single braid. She was wearing khaki pants, too, and a red pullover sweater.

Caryn was holding a red leash in one hand. At the end of the leash was a large golden-red dog with silky, slightly wavy fur.

"Sit, Sunny," said the girl in a quiet, pleasant voice. The dog sat down and looked around with a friendly expression on her face.

"Wow," said Violet.

The girl held out her hand. "How do you do, Mr. Alden?"

"I'm glad to see you again, Caryn," he answered, shaking her hand. "You won't remember this, but the last time I saw you, you were just a little girl. You've grown up, I see."

"I hope so," said Caryn, laughing a little.

Grandfather Alden bent over. "And this is Sunny," he said. He stroked the top of the dog's head. "She's a beauty."

Both Caryn and Mrs. Teague looked pleased. "Champion Gold Doubloon's Morning Sun," Mrs. Teague said. "That's her registered name. Of course, we call her Sunny."

"Well, let me introduce my family," said Grandfather. "These are my grandchildren, Henry, Jessie, Violet, and Benny."

Everyone shook hands. Then Benny held his hand out to Sunny.

"Benny, I don't think . . ." Grandfather began.

But Caryn smiled. "Shake, Sunny," she said.

Sunny held up her paw and shook hands with Benny.

"You're a smart dog!" cried Benny.

"Maybe you can teach Watch how to shake hands, Sunny. Watch is our dog. His full name is Watch Alden, but we call him Watch. He's smart, too."

Benny went to the front door and opened it. "Watch," he called. "Here, Watch!"

But Watch didn't come.

"He'll be here soon," said Benny confidently, closing the door.

Grandfather said, "Meanwhile, why don't we take you to your rooms and let you settle in. Then come down for something to eat and drink. You must be hungry after your trip."

"I have a special traveling kennel for Sunny," said Caryn. "May I set that up in my room? It's big enough for her to move around in and to keep her food and water in."

"Of course," said Grandfather. "Although she's so well-behaved, you don't need to keep her in there unless you want to."

It didn't take long for the Teagues to settle in. Soon they were all sitting around the kitchen table, eating fresh baked bread with butter and honey, and drinking milk or tea. Caryn had brought Sunny back down with her. When they'd reached the kitchen, she'd pointed to the corner by the door and said, "Down Sunny." Sunny had laid down. "Good girl. Stay," said Caryn. And Sunny had stayed there ever since.

"Does she do that at the shows?" asked Henry, looking admiringly at Caryn.

Caryn shook her head. "You're talking about obedience trials," she told Henry. "They're not part of this show. This show is about how a dog looks and acts. The judges look to see if it walks correctly and has the right color coat and the right kind of ears for its breed."

Violet looked puzzled. So did Jessie and Henry. Benny was twisting around in his chair looking for Watch, so he wasn't listening as intently as everyone else.

"At a show," Caryn explained, "each dog is walked around the ring while the judge watches. Then the judge looks at each dog more closely. The dog that's closest to perfect for its breed is the winner. So on the first day, Sunny will compete just against other golden retrievers."

"Oh," said Violet, looking less puzzled. "I think I see."

Caryn smiled. "And there's more. All the breeds of dogs are divided into seven different groups — Sporting Dogs, Non-sporting Dogs, Working Dogs, Herding Dogs, Terriers, Hounds, and Toys. Golden retrievers are in the Sporting Dog group. If Sunny is the best golden retriever, on the second day she'll compete against other kinds of sporting dogs, like Labrador retrievers and Irish setters."

"What if she's picked as the best in the Sporting Dog group?" Henry asked.

"Then on the last night she'll compete against the winners of the other six groups to see who is the best dog in the whole show."

"Wow," said Jessie. "The winner must be a terrific dog!"

"I can hardly wait to see all the dogs," said Violet.

"Yes," said Henry. "We're going to come watch the show and cheer for Sunny."

Caryn smiled at their enthusiasm. "Why don't you come to the show tomorrow?" she asked. "It doesn't really start until the day after, but people will be arriving and getting their dogs used to the place. It will be fun. There'll be a lot to see and do."

"That would be great!" said Henry.

Just then there was a scratching at the kitchen door.

"Watch!" exclaimed Benny happily. He rushed to the door and opened it.

Watch bounded in and stopped. His tail went up, and he started wagging it stiffly. The fur on the ruff of his neck stood up. As plainly as if he'd said it in English, he was asking, "Who is this strange dog in *my* kitchen?"

Sunny raised her head.

"Okay, Sunny," said Caryn. "Be good, now."

Sunny stood up. She and Watch touched noses. Gradually the fur on Watch's neck went down. Suddenly he put his two front legs flat on the floor, while sticking his hind-

quarters and tail up in the air. He wagged his tail furiously.

"He's saying, 'Let's play!' " Caryn laughed.

Everyone watched, smiling, as Sunny did the same thing as Watch.

"Would you like to go outside and play, Sunny?" asked Caryn.

"May we take them out, Grandfather?" asked Violet.

Grandfather laughed. "If it's okay with Mrs. Teague."

"Just be careful that Sunny stays in good shape for the show," said Mrs. Teague.

"Don't worry," Caryn said. "I'll keep an eye on Sunny. I'm sure nothing will happen to her."

"We'll show you our boxcar, too," said Henry. During their snack, they'd told the Teagues a little about their adventures in the old boxcar.

"I'd like that," said Caryn.

Everyone except Grandfather and Mrs. Teague went outside into the late afternoon sun. Watch and Sunny began to run in happy circles, barking and dancing around each other.

Henry led the way to the boxcar with Caryn walking beside him. Benny ran ahead and Jessie and Violet followed everyone.

Benny climbed up into the boxcar. "Look," he said, standing in the door. "This is my pink cup. I found it." The cracked pink cup was Benny's favorite possession. He had found it when they were all living in the old abandoned boxcar, and he still used it sometimes.

"It's a very nice cup," Caryn told Benny. She climbed into the boxcar after Benny and let the Aldens show her their former home, telling how Grandfather Alden had moved the boxcar to the backyard as a surprise, after they had come to live with him. Many of the things — the blue tablecloth, the kettle they'd cooked with, the old teapot and pitcher they'd found — were still inside.

"So this is the boxcar," Caryn said admiringly. "How lucky you were to find it! And brave to be on your own like that, too."

"It was fun," said Benny.

Henry smiled at his younger brother. "It *was* fun," he agreed. "But it was hard work, too. I'm glad we live with Grandfather Alden now."

"It's a wonderful boxcar," said Caryn. She and Henry sat down on the front stump and watched as the others romped and played with the two dogs until it was time for dinner.

CHAPTER 3

The Polka-Dotted Couple

The Greenfield Center, where the dog show was being held, was a big new building at the edge of town. As the Aldens approached it the next day, they could see cars and trucks and vans arriving, and people hurrying in and out. The sign out front read WELCOME TO THE FIRST ANNUAL GREENFIELD DOG SHOW.

"We've never been here before," said Henry.

"It's *big*," said Violet. "And there are so many people!"

"And dogs," said Benny.

They threaded their way among all the people and dogs and finally reached the back door.

"Look," said Violet, pointing. A sign by the door said REGISTRATION THIS WAY.

A moment later, Henry, who was the tallest, spotted Caryn. "There she is!" he said. He waved and Caryn waved back. She headed toward them, with Sunny walking sedately beside her.

"Hi Sunny!" said Benny happily. Sunny's tail waved gently to and fro.

"Sunny sure is calm around all these people," said Violet. Violet was shy, and being around a lot of people made her nervous.

Caryn smiled. "She's used to it. I've got her all signed in, but I'd like to walk around a little to get my bearings. Why don't you join me?"

"Okay," agreed Henry.

Together they all walked out to the main arena. It was bigger than a basketball court, with rows and rows of seats all around it. But velvet ropes had been strung across it, dividing it into sections.

"Each section is called a ring," Caryn explained. "That means that several different breeds of dogs will be shown at the same time in different rings of the arena. There will be a judge assigned to each ring."

"How do you know when it's your turn? And what ring to go in?" asked Jessie.

"The rings have numbers above them, see?" Caryn gestured. "And the time and ring number is listed in the program for the dog-show owners and handlers and the audience, and for the judges, too."

"It's a lot of work!" exclaimed Benny.

"That's true, Benny. But it's a lot of fun as well," Caryn said. She led them out of the arena.

Suddenly, a man and woman pushed past them, walking a beautiful white dog with black spots. The couple seemed to be dressed to match their dog — the man had on a black-and-white polka-dotted tie and the woman had on a black-and-white spotted dress.

The woman's face was red. "*Why* do we have to keep showing Zonker?" she demanded, grabbing the man's sleeve. "Tell me that! He's a champion now. Why not let him retire and have a little fun?"

"Because Zonker *likes* being a show dog," the man said angrily. "That's what he's bred and trained to do."

"*You* like it. That doesn't mean *Zonker* likes it!" the woman shouted angrily. "I'm tired of this whole dog-show business. For once I'd like to spend a few quiet weeks at home, instead of traveling around trying to win blue ribbons!"

"And *you'd* do anything to get what you want, wouldn't you!" the man shouted back, his own face growing red. "I think you'd actually sabotage a champion dalmation like Zonker — "

Just then, the two people seemed to realize

that others could hear their quarrel. They glanced over at Caryn and the Aldens. Then the woman hissed, "Shhh!" Without another word, the polka-dotted couple hurried out of sight with their dog.

"Maybe it's not so much fun for some people," said Benny.

Caryn sighed. "Maybe not, Benny."

They kept walking past a double door with a sign above it that said BENCHING AREA.

"What is a benching area?" asked Jessie.

"Come on, I'll show you," said Caryn. They pushed through the doors and saw long, wide, low benches. The benches were divided into sections and above each section was a sign.

"The signs are the names of the breeds of dogs," explained Caryn. "During the show, on the day your dog is being shown, you have to keep him or her in a special kennel in the section with other dogs of the same breed. Except when you're in the show ring, or exercising your dog, of course."

"Why?" asked Henry.

"Well, it's a good way for all the people showing dogs to get to know each other better, I guess. And visitors to the show can come and see the dogs up close, and ask questions. If you're interested in a particular breed of dog, like a golden retriever, it's a good way to find out more about it."

"There's the sign for the golden retrievers," said Violet.

"Oh, good. Now Sunny and I will know just where to go. Thank you, Violet," said Caryn.

"Oh no, oh no!" A small, round woman with big brown eyes was standing at a benching area nearby, wringing her hands.

Caryn looked up. "Mrs. DeCicco, what's wrong?"

"It's Ruth Chin," said Mrs. DeCicco. "You know, my assistant. She's usually so reliable. But she hasn't shown up yet. She was supposed to meet me here."

"I'm sure she'll be here at any moment," said Caryn soothingly. "Mrs. DeCicco, I'd like you to meet some friends of mine." Caryn introduced the Aldens to Mrs. DeCicco.

"What kind of dogs do you show?" asked Jessie.

"Beagles," said Mrs. DeCicco.

"Her beagles are famous," said Caryn.

Mrs. DeCicco smiled a little, but she was still obviously very worried.

Violet said, "Um, Mrs. DeCicco?"

"Yes, dear, what is it?" asked Mrs. De-Cicco, looking nervously around.

"Maybe we could help," said Violet.

Abruptly, Mrs. DeCicco looked back at Violet. "What?"

"Yes," said Henry. He put his hand on Violet's shoulder. "What do you need done? We could help until your assistant gets here."

"What a nice thought, dear, but . . . well
. . . well, maybe you could, at that!" She
studied the children thoughtfully for a
moment, then repeated, "Maybe you
could."

"They're very good with Sunny," Caryn
put in.

Mrs. DeCicco nodded. "Very well, then.
I'm staying at the Lamplighter Inn, just
down the road, where most of the show people are staying. If you could come this afternoon and help me exercise my dogs, I would
appreciate it."

"We'd be glad to," said Jessie.

"Lovely, lovely. Then I'll just leave
a message for Ruth at the information desk,
in case she shows up, and I'll meet you
at the inn this afternoon at four
o'clock."

"At four o'clock," repeated Henry carefully.

"Wow," said Benny. "We have a job at the
dog show."

Caryn smiled at Benny. "You sure do. I

think you'll enjoy it. Meanwhile, I think it's time for lunch for all of us."

"I like lunch," said Benny.

"Me, too, Benny," laughed Caryn. "Me, too."

CHAPTER 4

Dog Walking

The Lamplighter Inn seemed to be just as full of people and dogs and hustle and bustle as the Greenfield Center had been.

"How will we find Mrs. DeCicco?" asked Benny, staring.

"We'll ask at the desk," said Henry.

He led the way to the inn's front desk and asked for Mrs. DeCicco's room. Soon the Aldens were on their way to the north side of the inn.

"Here's her room," said Jessie. She knocked crisply on the door.

A few moments later, Mrs. DeCicco answered it. She looked just as flustered as before.

"Oh, good, I'm so glad you came. Ruth is *still* missing. It's not at all like her . . ." Mrs. DeCicco stepped back and motioned for the Aldens to come inside.

Along one side of the room were the dogs, in three large wire cages with flat metal bottoms. Each cage had a different blanket in it, along with dog toys and bowls for food and water. A small plaque above the door of each cage had the dog's name and the name *DeCicco Kennels*.

Mrs. DeCicco handed Violet, Henry, and Jessie each a leash, and began opening the cages. She lifted the first beagle out. "This is Sally. Good girl," she crooned as Sally wriggled and began to lick her face. Handing Sally to Henry, she reached for the next beagle. "Here's Gloria. She's Sally's mother." Gloria and Sally looked exactly alike. Jessie took Gloria and clipped the leash to the dog's collar as Henry had done with Sally.

"And this," said Mrs. DeCicco, opening

the last cage, "is Joe." She handed Joe to Violet.

"What about me?" asked Benny.

"You can carry their dog biscuits," said Mrs. DeCicco. "If they behave on their walk, you may give them each a dog biscuit at the end of it."

"Oh, good," said Benny. He took the three dog biscuits and put them carefully in his shirt pocket.

"Give them a brisk half-hour walk," instructed Mrs. DeCicco. "Don't let them dawdle too much." She had to raise her voice, for the beagles had begun to bay and leap up in excitement, and then to pull the children toward the door of the hotel room.

"See you in half an hour!" called Mrs. DeCicco as the Aldens and the beagles hurried out.

The Alden children didn't have to worry about getting the beagles to walk briskly. They trotted along the street in front of the hotel, heads down and ears flying, sniffing everything. People smiled and nodded as they passed, recognizing Mrs. DeCicco's prizewinners. One woman said, "Ah, the DeCicco beagles. Are you helping Mrs. DeCicco?"

"Yes we are," Henry said.

"It's too bad she didn't have a beagle for you to walk, too," the woman said, turning to Benny. She motioned to the little dog she was walking. "Would you like to walk Britty for a little while?"

"That would be great!" Benny said, looking down at the woman's long, skinny dog. "He looks like a hot dog!"

"He's a dachshund," the woman told him. "I'll wait for you here."

Benny took the leash and the children continued their walk. As they were passing the Greenfield Center, Benny exclaimed "Uh-oh!" and backed up into Jessie.

"What is it, Benny?" Jessie asked.

Benny pointed, his eyes round. A very big black-and-white spotted dog with a square head and pointed ears was being led on a leash toward them.

"Wow," breathed Violet. "That's a *huge* dog."

"Excuse me," said Henry. "What kind of dog is that?"

The tall, thin woman holding the dog's leash smiled down at them. "He's a Great Dane. We call him Berries. Because of his spots, you see?"

Berries lowered his head toward Benny and wagged his tail.

"Is he friendly?" Benny asked.

"Very. Great Danes are a very friendly breed," the woman said.

"I don't know . . ." Benny said, backing away nervously.

"How about if your brother holds his leash, and you can pat Berries," the woman offered.

Handing Sally's leash to Jessie, Henry took Berries's leash, feeling a bit nervous himself. But Berries stayed perfectly calm. Benny reached out and patted Berries's head. Berries lowered his head even more and his tail wagged harder.

"He likes that," the woman said. "Well, I think Berries and I had better be on our

way." Henry returned Berries's leash to her. "Come, Berries," she said.

After they had left, Benny turned to his sisters and brother. "He looked like he would be big and mean," said Benny.

"That just goes to show you can't judge by appearances," Henry said.

"Yes, but you should never pet strange dogs without asking their owners first," Jessie told Benny.

They had now gone all the way around the block, and they saw Britty's owner waiting for them.

"Thank you for letting me walk her," Benny said, giving her the leash.

"Thank *you*," the woman replied.

As they were heading back to the hotel, the Aldens passed lots of other people and dogs.

There were two full-coated collies being walked by a stately man with long, flowing golden hair, and a bulldog being walked by a thickset old man with a mashed-in nose.

"You know, some people look just like their dogs," whispered Violet.

"It's true," said Jessie. "Oh look! Excuse me, what kind of dog is that?"

A short, stout woman with very short, very white hair stopped and smiled at them, while her dog pulled on his leash and grinned a doggy grin. "She's an English bull terrier," said the woman. "Her name is Shug."

They all looked at Shug, who also had very short white hair and was very solidly built. "She looks like a nice dog," said Jessie politely.

"Oh, she is when she wants to be," said the woman cheerfully as Shug pulled her in the opposite direction.

Just then a large, shaggy dog bounded around from behind and stopped in front of them. It was clear from his excited wiggling that he wanted to play. He didn't have a tail, but his whole back end was wagging.

"A sheepdog!" cried Violet.

"An Old English sheepdog, actually," said a voice behind them. A man in a rumpled gray suit, with shaggy gray hair, came up to them.

"He's beautiful," said Violet.

"Thank you," said the man. "He's a champion — Champion Burger Plum Pudding."

"What a funny name," said Benny.

The man raised an eyebrow. "Burger is the name of my kennel where he was born and bred. Plum is from his father's name — Plum Best, you know — and Pudding is from his mother's name, Proof of the Pudding."

"Oh," said Benny. "Hello, Burger Plum Pudding." He began to pat the dog's head.

"I call him 'Plum' for short," said the man, smiling.

"Like Sunny!" said Benny.

"Sunny?" The man abruptly stopped smiling and his eyes narrowed. *"Sunny?"*

"That's the dog who's staying with us. She has a longer name, but the Teagues call her Sunny for short." Henry explained.

"The Teagues," repeated the man. "Well, well, well."

"Do you know the Teagues?" asked Jessie eagerly.

The man stared at them, then turned abruptly without answering. "Come, Plum," he ordered, and stalked away.

Plum hesitated. He liked having Benny pat his head.

"Now," ordered the man sharply.

Plum reluctantly obeyed.

"I wonder what that was all about," said Jessie, frowning as she watched the man march away with Plum trailing along behind him.

"I don't think he liked us," said Benny.

"He seemed to like us fine at first," said Henry, puzzled. "Until we mentioned Sunny. Oh, well, our half hour with these guys is almost up. We'd better get back. We don't want Mrs. DeCicco to worry."

"Do you think Sunny knows Plum?" asked Violet.

"We can ask tonight," said Jessie.

"I think that would be a very good idea!" agreed Henry.

"Is it a mystery?" asked Benny.

"Maybe it is, Benny," said Henry. "Maybe it is."

CHAPTER 5

The Mysterious Man

That night after dinner, as the Alden children sat on the wide front porch with their grandfather and the Teagues, Jessie said, "Mrs. Teague, do you know someone who has a dog named Plum?"

"Plum?" repeated Mrs. Teague. "Well, yes, I do. That's the name of a rather famous Old English sheepdog that is often at the same dog shows we attend."

"Yes. From Burger Kennels," said Caryn. "He's a lovely dog, friendly and gentle. A beautiful sheepdog."

"Why do you ask, Jessie?" Mrs. Teague inquired.

"We met Plum today while we were walking Mrs. DeCicco's beagles," explained Jessie.

Benny blurted out, "I liked Plum a lot. But I didn't like his owner."

"Oh, you must mean Lawrence Burger!" exclaimed Caryn.

"Mr. Burger didn't seem to like us very much," said Violet.

"At first he was nice," Henry put in. "But all of a sudden, he just turned and walked away."

"Yes. We were telling him about Sunny being in the dog show and he looked really upset," said Violet.

Caryn shook her head. "Plum is a lovely, wonderful dog, but I'm afraid Lawrence Burger is just the opposite."

"What do you mean?" asked Henry.

"He only wants to win. He's jealous of anybody else who wins. He's particularly jealous of Sunny because Sunny and Plum are often finalists for the Best of Show."

"Does Sunny win?" asked Benny.

"Sometimes Sunny wins," answered Caryn. "Sometimes Plum does. Sometimes other dogs do. But you know what's sad? Even when Plum wins, Lawrence never seems to enjoy it."

"It *is* too bad," said Mrs. Teague. "But some dog show people are like that, unfortunately."

"They think winning is everything?" asked Grandfather Alden.

"Exactly," said Mrs. Teague.

Caryn laughed softly. "I like winning, and so does Sunny. But I think Sunny likes other things, also."

"Like bones," guessed Benny.

"And playing," said Violet.

"And sleeping in the sun," suggested Jessie.

"Yes, all of those things — things I bet Plum likes, too. I hope someday Lawrence learns to enjoy life with Plum, instead of always worrying about winning," Mrs. Teague said.

"I hope so, too," said Benny.

Caryn smiled. "Well, it's time for Sunny to go to bed. It's a big day tomorrow and she needs her rest. And so do I!"

"So do we all," said Grandfather Alden, standing up. "Time for bed."

"I hope tomorrow hurries up and gets here," said Violet.

"It will be here soon, Violet," promised Grandfather Alden.

The next day, everyone in the Alden house was up early. The Teagues and Sunny left first. "We have to get to the benching area by eight-thirty," explained Caryn as they loaded Sunny and her equipment for the dog show into the car.

"We'll see you there *very* soon," Benny promised.

The Alden children hurried through breakfast. Then Grandfather drove them all to the Greenfield Center.

The center was even busier and more full of dogs than it had been the day before. The sound of barking filled the air. The loud-speaker boomed overhead. People hurried by in all kinds of clothes — some in aprons with pockets that held scissors and brushes, others in suits.

"The people in the aprons must be groomers," said Henry. "Caryn was explaining that they often work on combing and clipping the dogs to make them look as good as possible, right up to the moment they go in the ring!"

"That's a lot of work," Jessie said.

Henry explained more as they walked through the center. "There are rules about how dogs can be cut for the shows, too."

"It's funny, isn't it?" Violet gave a little skip. "Dogs get haircuts just like people do!"

Grandfather said, "Here are your ticket stubs. Our seats are in the middle over there. I'm going to buy a program for us and sit down. After you've looked around a little, why don't you come join me?"

"Okay, Grandfather," said Henry. "I'll put the tickets in my pocket where I can't lose them."

Grandfather went to find their seats around the show ring, while Henry, Jessie,

Violet, and Benny walked toward the benching area.

"Look, there's Mrs. DeCicco," said Henry. "Let's go say hello and wish her luck."

But as the Aldens got closer, they saw that Mrs. DeCicco was talking to three people wearing suits.

"Maybe we can wish her luck another time," said Violet shyly. Before the Aldens could leave, however, Mrs. DeCicco saw them and motioned them to come over.

"These are the Alden children, who helped me with my beagles last night when Ruth didn't show up. And these" — Mrs. DeCicco clasped her hands and almost bowed — "are some of the judges! They are some of *the* most important people at a dog show."

"Oh, now, I wouldn't say that," the tallest judge put in with a little shake of her head. "I'd say the owners and the handlers — and the dogs themselves — are the most important part of the show."

Mrs. DeCicco unclasped her hands and

wagged her finger. "No, no! Don't you believe it, children. These are *wonderful* judges. You know, I've been at shows where I've felt that the judges just didn't understand what a good beagle is. And of course my babies are perfect examples!" Mrs. DeCicco laughed and patted the tall judge's arm. The judge, looking uncomfortable, took a step backward as Mrs. DeCicco went on. "I know I can rely on you to choose the *best* dog."

All of the judges looked a little embarrassed at Mrs. DeCicco's gushing words. The tall judge cleared her throat and said, "We do our best." She turned to the Aldens. "Are you enjoying the dog show?"

The Alden children all smiled politely. "It's our first dog show," said Jessie. "We're having a lot of fun!"

The judges all smiled. "I'm glad," said the tall judge.

"Good luck to you, Mrs. DeCicco," said another judge, and the three judges moved away down the benching aisle.

As the judges left, Mrs. DeCicco nervously clasped her hands again. "Judges!" she said. "Oh, dear, oh dear."

"Is Ruth still missing?" asked Henry.

"What? Oh, no. She got here late last night. She'd had a flat tire. Strangest thing, you know. She'd just put new tires on her car." Mrs. DeCicco kept staring in the direction the judges had gone. "Oh, dear," she repeated. "I must win. I *must*."

"Mrs. DeCicco?" said Violet. "Winning isn't everything."

Mrs. DeCicco looked at Violet. "Maybe not. But if I don't win, I could lose everything!"

"What do you mean?" asked Jessie.

"I've put all my money, everything, into my beagles. And they all used to win all the time. But then I was in an accident and couldn't show my dogs for a long time. Now we have to start winning again soon, or I won't have any money left. I'll be forced to sell my dogs and my kennel!"

"Oh, dear," said Violet.

"I'm sure your beagles will win," said Henry.

With a sad, serious expression, Mrs. DeCicco said, "Do you think so? I hope you're right. They're such good dogs." She turned toward the three kennels with her beagles lined up inside. She bent down, and the sad expression left her face. "Aren't my beagles good boys and girls?"

The beagles began to bark happily. "Yes, *good* dogs, the best beagles in the world, no matter what," Mrs. DeCicco told them.

Henry looked at his watch. "We still have time to look around some more," he said. After saying good-bye to Mrs. DeCicco, the Aldens made their way through the benching area, still staring at all the different kinds of dogs and all their amazing shapes and sizes and colors.

Then Jessie said, "Look!"

At the very end of the row, a man was sneaking up to an unguarded kennel. He kept looking back over his shoulder nervously as he bent down. Inside the kennel, the Aldens could see a droopy-jowled basset hound growling angrily.

"Nice dog," said the man. The dog kept

growling, watching the man suspiciously.

"Good doggie," said the man. He appeared to be fumbling with the latch on the kennel door. The dog raised itself up on its front legs and barked. The man jerked his hand back.

"Excuse me," said Henry.

The man jumped and spun around. He was not much taller than Henry. He had brown wispy hair combed across the top of his almost bald head, heavy brown eyebrows, and sharp little blue eyes.

"Excuse me," Henry repeated. "Could we help you?"

"No!" said the man hastily. "Why do you ask?"

"Is that your basset hound?" asked Jessie.

"Why?" the man said.

"Because he doesn't seem to know you. If you were his owner, I don't think he'd bark at you like that," persisted Jessie.

"Okay, okay, so the dog isn't mine. A man can look at another person's dog, can't he?

It's a free country! Besides, I'm thinking of buying one. Yeah, that's it. Maybe this one. Now, if you kids will excuse mc — " With that, the man pushed past the Aldens and disappeared into the crowd!

CHAPTER 6

A Bad Haircut

The Aldens stared as the strange man hurried away.

"Do you think he was trying to steal that dog?" asked Violet.

Jessie put her hands on her hips. "I don't know. It sure looked like it. But how could he, in the middle of a dog show with so many people around?"

"With so many people, it might be easier," suggested Henry. "Everybody is busy with their own dog and not paying attention to other people's dogs. And there are so many people and so many dogs, no one really knows which person goes with which dog."

"I never thought about that," Jessie said thoughtfully. Violet and Benny nodded in agreement.

Just then, an announcement came over the loudspeaker: "Attention! The First Annual Greenfield Dog Show is about to begin!"

"We'd better hurry!" exclaimed Henry. The children walked hastily back through the benching area and went to join their grandfather. Mrs. Teague was already there with Grandfather Alden. Through binoculars, she was watching all the different breeds of dogs that were to be shown being led first into the arena and then to their show rings.

"Just in time," Grandfather said.

"Aren't you supposed to be with Sunny?" Violet asked as they all took their seats.

Mrs. Teague lowered her binoculars and leaned back. "I'll go to ringside when her breed, the golden retrievers, is about to be judged. Meanwhile, I'm going to enjoy the dog show from here, with all of you!"

Although they had already seen many,

many kinds of dogs in the benching area, the Aldens were amazed to see even more breeds of dogs being led into the rings. Mrs. Teague explained about all the different breeds and told them stories about some of the dogs she knew. One dog had saved her master's life by waking him up when a fire started in the hotel where he was staying. Another dog made visits to children who were sick in the hospital.

The Aldens watched and listened and applauded. At last it was time for the golden retrievers. Mrs. Teague hurried down to the ring as the beautiful golden dogs were being led in.

"Look, there's Caryn!" cried Jessica.

Caryn was wearing pants and a jacket that exactly matched Sunny's coat. She had on flat black shoes and a soft white blouse, and her golden hair was pulled back with a red bow.

"Caryn's all dressed up," Benny said. "She's as pretty as Sunny!"

The other Aldens laughed and Benny

laughed, too, although he wasn't sure why everyone was laughing.

The judge made a motion, and the handlers led their dogs in a circle around the ring. Then they all stopped at one side.

When the judge signaled, each handler and dog came forward, one pair at a time. The judge looked in each dog's mouth and ears and ran her hands over the dog's body. Afterwards, the handler walked the dog around the ring while the judge studied the way the dog moved and acted.

When Sunny's turn came, she stood proudly, her tail wagging slightly while the judge examined her. As Caryn led her in a circle around the ring, the Aldens clapped and cheered.

"I hope she wins," said Henry.

"She's the best dog, no matter what," said Violet loyally.

One by one the judge eliminated all the dogs except Sunny and a male golden retriever.

"He's a champion, too," said Jessie, studying her program.

The other dog finished his circle of the ring. Now the two dogs stood at attention at the side of the ring. The judge rubbed her chin. She walked back and forth between the two dogs. Then she made a motion for the dogs to walk around the ring again.

The two handlers led their dogs in a circle once more. As they passed the judge, she held up one finger to signal number 1, and pointed to Sunny, then two fingers and pointed to the other dog.

"Sunny won!" cried Henry.

"Hooray, hooray!" Benny shouted. They applauded as the judge handed a big blue ribbon to Caryn. Photographers took pictures of the new Greenfield Dog Show Champion Golden Retriever from every angle.

The Aldens watched as Caryn led Sunny out of the ring. Mrs. Teague hugged Caryn first, and then Sunny.

"Let's go down and meet the Teagues and

Sunny in the benching area," suggested Grandfather Alden.

"Oh, boy," said Benny. Hopping up and down with excitement, he led the way out of the viewing stands and back to the benching area where the golden retrievers were staying.

On their way, they saw two familiar faces. "Woof," said a friendly dog voice.

"Oh, it's Plum," said Violet, reaching out to pat the eager sheepdog's head.

"Congratulations," said an icy voice that didn't sound as if it meant the word at all.

At the other end of Plum's leash stood Lawrence Burger. "I see your little friend Sunny won," he said.

"Thank you," said Jessie politely.

"I hope Plum wins, too," said Benny.

Lawrence Burger smiled a cold smile. "Do you? Somehow, I doubt that. Come along, Plum."

The two walked away.

"What a strange man," said Henry. "Come on, let's go find Sunny — "

Just then, there was a horrible shriek.

Everyone stopped and turned to stare in the direction of the sound.

A man came running by, leading a big white poodle on a leash. "Look! Look what someone has done to my beautiful Curly!" he shrieked.

"Oh, look," gasped Violet. "Poor dog!"

Curly's beautiful, curly white coat had been shaved into ragged stripes.

A dog show official came hurrying up with a security guard. The security guard began to ask the man questions while the official tried to calm him down.

"I don't know *when* it happened," the man said. "I took Curly to have a little touch-up grooming, just after he won the poodle competition. Then I got a message that I had a phone call. But when I got to the information booth, there was no one on the phone. I was on my way back when I met my groomer going to the information booth. He said *he'd* gotten an urgent message to meet me there. I told him I never sent such a message. When we got back, we found Curly on the grooming table — like *this*!"

"Have you noticed any suspicious characters hanging around your dog?" asked the security guard.

"There's a suspicious character!" Henry nudged Jessie. Sure enough, there was the man they had seen near the basset hound's kennel. As they watched, the man disappeared into the crowd.

"No," moaned Curly's owner. "I didn't notice anyone suspicious. "Oh, this is awful. Now Curly's chances of winning the Best in Show are ruined. *Ruined*!"

"Look, Mrs. DeCicco," cried Benny, as Mrs. DeCicco passed nearby. "Look at Curly!"

But Mrs. DeCicco didn't seem to hear Benny or notice the poodle. She walked right by, as if she didn't want to be connected to the incident in any way.

"That's odd," said Jessie. But before she could say anything else, Grandfather said, "We'd better go find the Teagues and Sunny."

By the time the Aldens joined them, the

Teagues had already heard about what had happened. Sunny was lying in her kennel, which had a big blue ribbon fastened to it, eating a dog biscuit and looking unconcerned. But Mrs. Teague and Caryn were plainly shocked.

"Who would do such an awful thing?" asked Caryn.

"And why?" asked Henry.

"Maybe it was a joke," Benny suggested. He added, "A *bad* joke."

"Whoever did it was a bad person, Benny," said Jessie. "But I don't think it was a joke."

"Maybe someone did it to eliminate the competition. You know, if Curly can't compete, maybe someone else has a better chance of winning," said Violet.

Henry nodded. "Yes! Maybe the person whose poodle came in second did it. That makes them first now, doesn't it?"

"I'm not sure." Caryn frowned. "But the poodle who came in second, the reserve champion, is owned by a very honest

woman. I'm sure she would never do something like that. She's a good person, and she
loves dogs."

"That's true," Mrs. Teague said. She
shook her head and sighed. "Oh, well. I sup-
pose on the bright side of things, Curly will
get a little vacation now while his coat grows
back. He's been a show dog for a long time
and has won almost everything a dog can
win. Maybe he'll like getting to stay at home
and enjoy a different life."

The Alden children exchanged glances.
They were all remembering the couple they
had overheard arguing the first day of the
show. And they were all wondering if shav-
ing Curly was the sort of thing someone would do because they believed dogs
shouldn't be in dog shows.

"Could it have been that woman who was
arguing that her dog Zonker should be al-
lowed to quit being a show dog?" asked Jessie
aloud.

"Or Mr. Burger?" suggested Violet. "He's
such a mean man."

"He can't be all mean, can he?" asked Henry. "Or how could he have a dog as nice as Plum?"

Jessie lowered her voice. "What if it was Mrs. DeCicco? She really needs to win badly. And she was *right there*."

"I can't believe Mrs. DeCicco would do something like that!" exclaimed Violet.

"Time to go," said Grandfather Alden. He turned to Mrs. Teague. "But we'll be back tomorrow to see Sunny win again!"

"Is the Best Dog in Show contest tomorrow, Grandfather?" asked Benny as they left the Greenfield Center.

"No, that's the night after tomorrow, Benny," Grandfather explained. "Remember when Caryn said that all the breeds of dogs are divided into seven different groups?"

Benny looked puzzled.

"Sunny is in the Sporting Dog group, remember?" Jessie said.

"Y-yes." Benny still looked as puzzled as he sounded.

"Well, tomorrow Sunny will compete against the other sporting dogs to see who is the very best sporting dog."

"Oh," said Benny. "I think I see . . . when Sunny wins tomorrow, will she be the best sporting dog at the dog show?"

"Yes, Benny!" Henry said. "Then, the next night, the best dog in each group — Herding, Sporting, Working, Terrier, Hound, Non-sporting and Toy — will compete to see who is the best dog in the *whole* show."

"Okay," said Benny. He gave a little skip. "Can we come see Sunny win tomorrow night and the next night, too?"

Grandfather Alden laughed, but before he could answer, they saw Plum and his owner again.

"Oh, look," said Violet. "Plum won the blue ribbon!"

Sure enough, Mr. Burger was holding a blue ribbon and looking very pleased.

"Congratulations!" called Jessie.

"Thank you!" said Mr. Burger. Then he

saw who had said it, and his smile froze. He turned on his heel and marched Plum in the other direction.

Watching them go, Violet shook her head. "I don't like Mr. Burger very much. But *Plum* is a nice dog."

CHAPTER 7

A Surprise for Sunny

"I want to make a surprise for Sunny," announced Benny the next morning after the Aldens and the Teagues had finished breakfast and Grandfather had taken the Teagues on a tour of Greenfield. Benny and his brother and two sisters had gone to their boxcar. Violet and Henry were sweeping it out and dusting it while Jessie and Benny oiled a squeaky hinge on the boxcar door and fixed a rickety leg on the table.

"A surprise, Benny? What kind of a surprise?" asked Violet.

"Something special for when Sunny wins the whole show," Benny told her. He frowned, thinking hard. "Maybe a chocolate cake."

Henry laughed and shook his head. "Sunny might like chocolate cake, Benny, but I don't think it would be very good for her."

"Oh, yes," said Benny. "I remember Mrs. Teague telling us that chocolate could make dogs very, very sick." His eyes widened at the awful thought of not being able to eat chocolate.

Violet had been thinking hard, too. Suddenly she clapped her hands together. "I know! We could make a flag for Sunny, or a banner, to wave at the show for her when she wins!"

Benny clapped his hands together, too. "Yes! A beautiful, *big* banner!"

Violet reached up and pulled a shoebox off one of the shelves in the boxcar. "We still have paints in here from the time we made signs for our helper service," she said. She studied the contents of the box thoughtfully and said, "But not enough to make a really *great* banner."

"Well, we're almost finished here," said Henry. "As soon as we do, let's ride our bicycles into town and get some more art supplies."

"Good idea," said Jessie. She checked the leg on the table one last time to make sure that it wasn't loose anymore and then stood up. "We can get a long roll of paper for the banner."

"We need some way to hold it up, too," said Violet. "Maybe a stick or pole — sort of like a short flagpole — at each end, so we can raise it up high."

Henry added, "Yes, and we could roll the banner up from each end, then. That would make it easy to carry without tearing it."

"I get to hold one end of the banner, don't I?" demanded Benny.

"You and I will hold one end, Benny, and Violet and Jessie can hold the other," answered Henry.

"Okay," Benny agreed.

As quickly as they could, the Aldens finished their work in the boxcar. Soon they were on their bicycles riding into town to get supplies to make a banner for Sunny.

In the art supply store, they found just the right roll of paper for making a long banner. Benny picked out some gold paint for writing Sunny's name on the banner. "It sort of matches her coat," he explained.

But they couldn't find poles to attach to the ends of the banner.

"Why don't you try the hardware store," suggested the owner of the art supply store. "Maybe a yardstick would be just the thing."

"A yardstick! That might work. Thank you," said Henry.

Carrying their supplies, the Aldens went into the hardware store. Inside, they found all kinds of sticks and poles, flat and round, used for building things. "This is great," said Jessie holding up a thin, smooth, round wooden pole that was almost as long as she was tall. "It's called a *dowel*. I wonder what it is used for?"

"I don't know, but look at this green pole. It's used for staking up tomatoes and peas and beans in gardens," said Henry.

"Both of those would work," said Violet.

"Here are the yardsticks!" cried Benny. He held up two yardsticks, with the flat sides marked out into feet and inches. "Why are they called yardsticks?"

"Because they are three feet long. That's a yard," explained Violet.

"Oh," said Benny. He waved the sticks. "I like these. Let's use the yardsticks."

"It would probably be easier to attach the banners to the flat sides of the yardstick," said Jessie, putting the dowels down reluctantly.

"True," said Henry. "Yardsticks it is, Benny."

"Good." Still holding the yardsticks up high, Benny led the way down the aisle to the cash register. But at the end of the aisle he stopped and pointed one of the yardsticks in front of him. "Look," he whispered loudly. "There's the polka-dot woman! The one with the dog named Zonker!"

Sure enough, ahead of them at the counter was the woman who owned Zonker. Today she was wearing a black-and-white spotted jumpsuit. But Zonker wasn't with her. Instead, she was lifting a small black-and-white spotted cat out of a battered cat carrier held together with tape and wire, and into a new heavy-duty plastic carrier. "Thank goodness you had one of these," she said. "Spike was about to tear up his old one! We always travel with him, you know. He and our dog, Zonker, are best friends."

The hardware store owner smiled. "You got the last one. Looks like it's time to order some new ones."

"Thank you again," said the woman, picking up the cat carrier and carrying it out of the store. The cat inside poked his paw out and began batting at the latch. "Oh, no you don't Spike," they heard her say as she pushed the hardware store door open. "That's a special latch. It's catproof!"

"Wow," said Benny. "A cat and a dog are *best* friends. Did you hear that?"

"It is funny, isn't it," said Jessie as they made their way to the counter and paid for the two yardsticks. "Most dogs don't like cats, and most cats don't like dogs."

"I guess some cats — and some dogs — are different," said Henry, laughing.

They went back to the boxcar and unrolled the paper carefully.

"Let's draw a picture of Sunny," said Benny. "And Watch."

Watch stood with his paws on the edge of the boxcar door, watching them.

"We can do Sunny at one end and Watch at the other," agreed Violet.

"What do we write on the banner, Benny?" asked Jessie.

"Hooray for Sunny!" answered Benny promptly.

"Good," said Henry. "It will look great!"

Working together, they carefully drew pictures of Sunny and Watch. Then, as Violet and Benny painted the pictures, Henry and Jessie wrote in big, bright letters, *Hooray for Sunny!* At last they were finished. They all stepped back to admire their work.

"It looks just like Sunny. And Watch, too," said Henry.

"I know," said Benny proudly.

They all laughed. Just then, they heard Mrs. McGregor's voice. "Lunchtime!" she called.

"We'll put the yardsticks on when it's dry, after lunch," said Jessie.

"It's a beautiful poster," said Benny. "See? I even put gold stars around Sunny and Watch."

"It *is* a beautiful poster, Benny," said Violet.

Pleased with their morning's work, the Aldens hurried back to the house to wash their hands and have their lunch.

CHAPTER 8

An Unexpected Visitor

At last it was evening, time to go to the dog show. The Aldens had finished the banner and put it carefully away, until the next night when they felt sure Sunny would compete for Best in Show. Then they'd gotten dressed up and gone to the Center. They saw that everyone else was dressed up for the evening's judging, too. Some of the handlers were wearing long dresses or dark suits. One man even had on a tuxedo. Excitement was in the air.

Mrs. DeCicco was dressed up, too. She was wearing a short, glittery dress with silvery high-heeled shoes.

"You look great, Mrs. DeCicco," Benny told her.

Mrs. DeCicco seemed startled for a moment as if she were surprised to see them. Then she smiled. "Thank you, Benny," she said. "I think this dress will stand out in the show ring, don't you? It doesn't hurt to catch the judge's attention, you know."

"Why are you carrying scissors?" asked Benny.

"Scissors?" Mrs. DeCicco looked down at the small scissorlike instrument in her hand.

"Oh!" exclaimed Violet. "Those aren't scissors, are they? They're grooming clippers. Remember, the groomer who was working on Curly had grooming clippers just like that."

"Do you trim the beagles?" asked Jessie. "They don't seem to have much hair to trim."

Mrs. DeCicco looked startled again, and then a little uncomfortable and embarrassed. "Well," she said, "Er, actually, don't tell anyone, but I was just on my way to do a little trimming on my own hair. My bangs are a little too long, and these are much sharper than ordinary scissors, you know! I keep them just for me." With an embarrassed little laugh, she waved and left.

"Euuw," said Jessie. "Dog scissors!"

"She just uses them for her own hair, Jessie. You heard her," Violet said. "She doesn't need them for the beagles."

"I think it's sort of suspicious, anyway," said Henry. "Maybe that's not why she has them at all."

"Do you think *she* was the one who clipped Curly?" asked Violet.

"I don't know," said Henry. "Maybe. . . ."

Just then, Grandfather said, "There's Mrs. Teague. Come on, everybody." The Alden children followed their grandfather into the stands to join their friend.

"Oh, look! We have ringside seats," said Jessie as the Aldens sat down. "This is great!"

Mrs. Teague nodded, looking pleased by Jessie's excitement. "They always give the winners the best seats for the final judgings."

"Thank you for inviting us," said Violet, and the others joined in with their appreciation.

"I'm glad you could be here," Mrs. Teague added. "It is wonderful for Sunny to have her own cheering section."

"Hooray for Sunny!" cried Benny.

Everyone laughed. "Not yet, Benny," said Jessie. "But soon."

"Look!" said Henry. "Here comes the first group of dogs."

"The terriers," said Mrs. Teague. She pointed to a small dog with a short tail and pointed face. "That's the fox terrier champion, called Chaser. He's favored to win the best of the terrier group."

"If he wins, that means he'll compete for best dog in the whole show, Benny," Violet explained.

Benny nodded seriously.

Even the judges were more dressed up that night. The judge of the terrier group had on a tuxedo with a red cummerbund and a red bow tie. He had rosy cheeks and little round glasses that he kept pushing up on his short, turned-up nose.

The dogs walked into the ring. An expectant hush fell over the audience.

Suddenly Chaser lunged to the end of his leash and began barking hysterically!

The square black Scottish terrier next to him did the same thing!

Then all the dogs began to jump and bark. One dog pulled loose from her handler and ran across the ring, knocking over a small table before anyone could catch her. Two other dogs got their leashes tangled as they leaped and struggled to get free. Shouts of surprise filled the Greenfield Center.

"Oh no!" cried Violet. "Look!"

A very frightened black-and-white spotted cat was dodging across the arena, skittering away from each dog, and from the people who were now trying to catch him.

"Look over there! By the entrance! Isn't that the same man we saw yesterday? At the basset hound cage?" said Henry.

"Where? I don't see anyone," said Jessie.

"Come on!" said Henry as the cat darted

between the legs of the officials. "That cat needs help!"

The Alden children jumped out of their seats and hurried to the stairs leading to the arena floor.

The small black-and-white form streaked by.

"He's heading for the benching area!" gasped Henry. "We'd better catch him before he gets back there."

The children raced down the corridor just in time to see the cat dodge through an open door that said FIRST AID. A young man in a white coat who had been sitting by the door jumped up in surprise.

"Was that a *cat*?" he asked in amazement.

"Yes," panted Violet. "We have to catch him."

"Quick, go inside!" said the young man. "I'll close the door!"

"Thanks," said Henry as the children hurried by the young man and into the small first aid room.

Benny bent down and looked under the narrow bed on one side of the room. "There he is. He's hiding under the bed."

"Oh, poor kitty," said Violet. "He must be so scared. We should be very quiet and let him calm down."

The Aldens sat down on the floor, and Violet began to talk softly to the frightened cat. At last the cat let her reach under the bed and pick him up.

Violet looked puzzled. "You know, this cat looks like Spike — the cat we saw in the hardware store with the polka-dot woman."

"You're right!" exclaimed Henry.

Violet looked even more puzzled. "But how did he get loose at the dog show?"

"I don't know," said Henry, "but we'd better get him out of here now!"

Benny patted the cat's head.

"Oh, good, you caught him," said the young man. "I've been a nurse for a while now. But it's the first time I've ever had a cat in the first aid room!"

"What do we do now?" asked Benny.

"Maybe we should find the polka-dot woman, and ask her if this is her cat," said Jessie.

"Or we could take him to the Greenfield Animal Shelter," Violet suggested. "They'll know how to find his owner. He has a collar."

"But we can't go now," said Henry. "We have to see Sunny compete."

"I have an idea," Jessie said. "Wait here." She ran down the corridor toward the benching area. A few minutes later she hurried back, holding a small animal carrier. It had air holes in the side and a screen door that latched shut in the front.

"That's perfect," said Violet. "We can put the cat in here until after the show, then take it to the shelter."

"Where did you get the carrier?" asked Henry.

"Mrs. DeCicco," said Jessie, trying to catch her breath. "She said she just happened to have an extra one. I ran into her right outside. She said she always brings extra travel kennels for her beagles. She said we could bring it back tomorrow."

Carefully, Violet slipped the black-and-white cat into the carrier. Then they took the cat back with them and put the carrier on the floor at their feet.

"You did a good job," said Grandfather.

"Yes." Mrs. Teague smiled. "And you still have time to watch the judge finish the terrier group. It took a little while to get everyone settled down."

As the children watched, it became clear that some of the terriers were still upset by all the commotion caused by the cat. One small, bouncy terrier kept turning its head all around instead of looking straight ahead as it was led in a circle around the ring. Other terriers kept barking as they stood waiting their turn. The owners looked even more upset than the dogs. And Chaser kept pulling on his leash.

Mrs. Teague shook her head as she watched Chaser. "That's not good," she commented.

At last the judge chose the best of the terriers. But it wasn't Chaser. It was the white bull terrier who won.

There were gasps from the audience when the judge announced her choice. "It's an upset victory for the bull terrier," said Mrs. Teague.

"That's Shug!" said Violet. "Remember that bull terrier we met when we were walking Mrs. DeCicco's beagles?"

"Yes!" the other children said. They applauded as the terriers were led out of the ring.

When Sunny's turn came, they applauded even louder.

"How can the judge not see she's the very best!" whispered Violet.

"The other dogs are good, too," said Henry, trying to be fair.

It was true. The black labrador retriever was obviously a champion. He walked confidently around the ring, his head held high, causing the judge to nod approvingly. And a beautiful Irish setter with a gleaming red coat won a loud round of applause from the spectators.

"Oh, dear," said Violet. They all cheered extra loud when Sunny's turn came.

The judge motioned for the Sporting Group to circle once more. Then she had all the dogs line up again. Slowly, she walked up and down the line.

She stopped in front of the labrador.

She stopped in front of Sunny.

She stepped back and raised one finger for first place — and pointed at Sunny!

"She's going to win Best in Show! I just know it!" said Henry as Caryn and Sunny stood proudly in the center of the ring accepting their award.

"I think you're right," said Jessie.

At last the judging was over. The Aldens took the cat to the animal shelter, where the night attendant let them in.

"We'll take good care of him," the attendant promised. "Meanwhile, I bet he'd like some food and water, wouldn't you, fella?" He lifted the cat out of the carrier and handed the carrier to Jessie. Then, holding the cat in his arms and talking to him, the attendant carried him to the back of the shelter where the cats were kept.

"How do you think the cat got in the dog show?" asked Henry as Grandfather drove them home.

"I wouldn't go to a dog show if I was a cat," Benny said sleepily, leaning against Grandfather's shoulder.

"Do you think someone did it on purpose?" Violet wondered aloud. "Like that mean trick they played on Curly?"

"Well, however the cat got in the Greenfield Center, he sure upset all the terriers. Chaser, the dog favored to win, was so upset that he *didn't* win," Henry pointed out.

"Someone had to have let that cat in," agreed Jessie. "But who? And why?"

But no one could think of any answers.

CHAPTER 9

Sunny Disappears

The next day, the last day of the Greenfield Dog Show, was bright and clear. Since Watch couldn't go to the dog show, and since he had to go to the veterinarian's that afternoon to get his shots (although of course, *he* didn't know it), the Aldens decided to take him for a special walk in the park. As Watch ran and sniffed happily, the four of them discussed all the mysterious things that had been happening.

"It's as if someone is trying to ruin the whole dog show," said Henry. "But why?"

They all watched silently for a moment as Watch sniffed at something under a tree. He cocked his head and started to dig furiously.

Then Jessie went on thoughtfully, "First we see that suspicious-looking man at the basset hound's cage, and he doesn't even have a good reason for being there . . ."

"And then someone shaves poor Curly the poodle," put in Violet.

Nodding, Jessie went on, "And that's when we saw that same man again."

"But we saw Mrs. DeCicco then, too. She pretended not to see us, remember?" said Henry.

"Maybe she really *didn't* see us," objected Violet. "She's got a lot on her mind."

"Maybe," said Henry doubtfully. "Anyway, don't forget that we also saw Mrs. DeCicco with those grooming scissors. It's hard to believe she'd really use them to trim her bangs."

"And she did have that extra carrier when the cat was let out," said Jessie.

"But it looked like that cat we saw with the polka-dot woman," said Benny.

"I know." Jessie bit her lower lip, thinking hard. "We called the shelter this morning. No one has claimed the cat yet, and we haven't seen the polka-dot woman to find out if that cat is hers."

"It could be," said Henry. "We heard her say she doesn't think Zonker should have to keep going to dog shows. So maybe she is trying to sabotage the whole dog show."

Jessie said, "That's true. Or maybe it's Mrs. DeCicco. Maybe she is trying to make sure she wins. She said she has to win or she'll lose everything."

"But she's so nice," said Violet.

"Remember that Great Dane?" asked Benny suddenly. "He looked mean, but he was nice. You said you can't tell by looking at someone."

"You're right, Benny." Violet sighed.

"What about Mr. Burger?" said Benny. He picked up a stick. "Here, Watch!" he called and threw the stick. Watch stopped digging and ran to look for the stick. "Mr. Burger's mean, and he thinks winning is the most important thing."

"Just because he's mean doesn't mean he'd sabotage a whole dog show," said Henry. "Besides, we haven't seen him around when any of this has been happening. And unlike Mrs. DeCicco, he's not going to lose *everything* if he loses."

"Don't forget the mysterious man, either," said Jessie. She paused, then added, "Maybe it is Mr. Burger! Maybe he and the mysterious man are working together!"

"Or the mysterious man and Mrs. De-Cicco. Or the polka-dot woman," said Henry.

"Come on, Watch, time to go back," called Violet. The Aldens walked slowly through the park and back down the street. When they reached home, they were no nearer to solving the mystery.

That afternoon, before Watch's appointment, they went to the center to see how Sunny and Caryn were doing. The feeling of excitement that had been in the air the night before was even stronger.

"Let's find Caryn quick and wish her good luck," said Benny.

But before they could find Caryn, she found them.

"Caryn, what's wrong?" asked Jessie as Caryn hurried toward them.

"It's Sunny," gasped Caryn, her face pale. "She's gone!"

"*Gone?* What do you mean?" asked Henry.

Caryn took a deep breath to try and calm herself. But her voice was shaky as she answered, "She's disappeared. One minute she was in her kennel, with her chin on her favorite toy, and the next minute . . ."

"You mean she got out of her kennel?" asked Violet. "Is she lost?"

"No! At least, I don't think so." Caryn looked around as if Sunny might come walking toward them. "No, it's impossible for her to open her kennel by herself. Someone had to have let her out!"

"Another mean trick," gasped Violet.

Henry patted Caryn's hand. "She can't have gone far. Someone would have seen her wandering around and recognized her, wouldn't they?"

"I don't know," said Caryn. "My mother

and I asked everybody who'd been around us if they'd seen anything, but they're all so busy that no one was paying any attention. Mrs. DeCicco had stopped by to say hi a little earlier. She did say she thought she saw someone sort of hanging around nearby. But she can't remember what he looked like."

Caryn let go of Henry's arm and clasped her hands together. "Oh, dear, oh, dear. All I did was walk to the end of the aisle to fill Sunny's water dish. How could there have been time for her to get out? Or for someone to let her out!"

"We'll find her," said Henry reassuringly. "We can divide up and look."

Jessie and Benny, Violet and Henry, and Caryn all went to look for Sunny. But when the three search parties met back at Sunny's empty kennel half an hour later, no one had found her, or found anyone who remembered seeing her.

"Did she have on a collar?" asked Henry. "Maybe she got out of the center somehow and someone will find her around town."

"Sunny wasn't wearing a collar," said

Caryn. She seemed a little calmer, but she was still pale with worry. "She's been tatooed on her inner thigh with a registration number — many show dogs are — but I didn't have her collar on her."

Henry looked serious. "I guess some people wouldn't know to look for a registration number," he said.

"No, but every veterinarian does, and every animal shelter," said Caryn.

"Why don't we call the Greenfield Animal Shelter and see if they've found her?" suggested Violet.

"Good idea," said Henry. He hurried toward the phone booths. But he returned shortly, shaking his head. "No Sunny," he said. "I left a description in case anyone did turn in a lost golden retriever." He started to say something else, then stopped.

"I just remembered, we have to take Watch to Dr. Scott's," Jessie said.

"That's right," said Henry quickly. He looked at Caryn. "We have to go now," he said. "But we'll come back as soon as we can to help you keep looking."

Caryn smiled bravely. "Thank you," she said. "I'd better go file a report."

"See you in a little while," said Henry.

"We'll find Sunny. I know we will," Violet told Caryn.

As the Aldens hurried home, Henry said, "I didn't want to say anything in front of Caryn, but when I called the shelter, I was told that someone had claimed the black-and-white cat."

"Who?" asked Benny.

"A very angry woman. And she was wearing — "

"Black-and-white spots," guessed Jessie.

"Right," said Henry. "She told the attendant at the animal shelter that someone had *stolen* the cat out of her hotel room last night while she and her husband and Zonker were at the dog show."

"Wow," said Violet softly.

The Aldens were quiet as they got Watch and walked to Dr. Scott's office. At last Benny broke the silence. "Do you think someone stole Sunny, too? Do you think there's a petnapper?"

Jessie looked grim. "It sure seems that way."

"Mrs. DeCicco? She was right there," said Henry.

"Not Mrs. DeCicco," cried Violet. She put her hands in her pockets and shook her head.

"But she's been around when everything has happened. And don't you think it is a little suspicious that she just happened to have an extra carrier with her? Maybe that's what she used to bring the cat into the show in the first place," reasoned Harry.

They turned the corner and walked down the road to the veterinarian's.

"I think it was the suspicious man," said Violet. "He was outside the basset hound's kennel. Maybe he was going to steal the basset hound, and instead he stole Sunny!"

"But then why would he bring a cat into the show? Or shave Curly?" asked Jessie.

"I don't know," said Violet, wrinkling her brow. "Could it be the polka-dot woman? Would she be mean enough to let her own cat loose at a dog show?"

"It's mean Mr. Burger," insisted Benny. "I don't like him."

Hearing the tone of Benny's voice, Watch barked in agreement and pulled on his leash.

"Whoa, boy," said Violet.

"Just because you don't like someone doesn't mean he's bad, Benny. But you're right to suspect him, I think," said Jessie. "He wants to win. With Sunny out of the way, his chances are better." She added thoughtfully, "So are Mrs. DeCicco's."

"It really is almost like someone is trying to sabotage the Greenfield Dog Show," said Henry.

"Maybe that is it," said Violet.

"All the bad luck things that have been happening *have* happened to the whole dog show. But why would anyone want to ruin a dog show?" asked Jessie.

"Maybe it's someone who doesn't like dogs," Benny said.

"Here's Dr. Scott's office," said Violet.

Watch knew where he was. His ears went down and his tail drooped. He planted all four feet firmly on the sidewalk and refused to move. At last Violet had to bend over, pick him up, and carry him inside.

Dr. Scott smiled kindly when she saw Watch. "There's a good boy," she said, checking him out. The way she looked in his mouth and ears and ran her hands over him was sort of the same way the judge handled dogs in the show.

"Now," said Dr. Scott, "who will hold Watch while I give him his shots?"

Benny closed his eyes shut and grabbed Violet's hand. Soft-hearted Violet shook her head and looked away.

"Henry and I will," said Jessie.

"Hang on now," Dr. Scott said.

But it turned out they didn't have to hold on tight at all. Dr. Scott was such a good veterinarian that Watch hardly seemed to feel his shots.

Very soon Dr. Scott said, "All done."

Benny opened his eyes and they all began to pet and praise Watch, telling him what a good, brave dog he was.

"Here," said Dr. Scott. She reached in a jar on the counter and pulled out a small dog biscuit. Jessie lifted Watch down onto the floor, and Dr. Scott gave him the biscuit. He munched on it happily.

As Watch ate his biscuit, the Aldens asked Dr. Scott about her vacation.

"It was a good vacation," Dr. Scott told them. "But I'm glad to be back. What's been happening while I was away?"

"The dog show!" exclaimed Benny. He pulled on Dr. Scott's sleeve. "May I go visit the dogs who are staying with you?"

"Yes, Benny, you may," said Dr. Scott. "My assistant is back there now."

"Thank you," said Benny, and he went to visit the dogs.

Dr. Scott turned to Jessie, Violet, and Henry. "I have tickets for tonight," said Dr. Scott. "Do you like dog shows?"

"We have one of the dogs staying with us," said Jessie. "Or we used to, until she disappeared!"

"Disappeared?" asked Dr. Scott. "What happened?"

So the Aldens told Dr. Scott all about Sunny and how she had disappeared from the dog show that morning, and about all the other mysterious things that had happened.

"I don't know. It could be that someone *is* trying to sabotage the dog show," Dr. Scott said thoughtfully. "Although I can't imagine why. Whatever is going on, someone is up to no good!"

"We've got to find Sunny," said Henry. "So she can win best in show tonight."

"But we don't know where else to look — " began Violet.

"Sunny, Sunny, Sunny!" cried Benny. He came barreling back into the examining room and skidded to a stop. He pointed back toward Dr. Scott's kennels. "Sunny is back there!"

"Benny, it can't be Sunny. What would she be doing at Dr. Scott's?" asked Henry.

"It is Sunny, it is," insisted Benny. "I knew who she was and she knew me, too!"

Jessie shook her head. "I know you want to find Sunny as badly as the rest of us do, Benny, but. . . ."

"Do you have a golden retriever staying with you, Dr. Scott?" Violet asked.

"As a matter of fact someone just brought one in," Dr. Scott said. "Would you like to see her?"

"It's Sunny," Benny said stubbornly.

"Come on, Benny. We'll all go see," said Violet.

Swallowing the last bit of his biscuit, Watch trotted after them, with Henry holding his leash. But when they got to the kennels, Watch barked excitedly and pulled the leash out of Henry's hand. He raced up to one of the dog runs and began pawing at the gate. On the other side of the gate, a beautiful golden retriever began barking and pawing, too.

"I don't believe it," said Henry. "Could that be Sunny?"

"Sunny," said Violet as they went up to the gate. "Sunny?"

The golden retriever leaped up excitedly.

"A man brought her in this morning," said Dr. Scott.

"Can you describe him?" asked Jessie.

"He was round. He had sort of shaggy gray hair, and it looked as if he had slept in his clothes, they were so wrinkled. That's really all I remember, but I would know him if I saw him again. He signed his name as Mr. Smith. He just wanted to board her overnight," said Dr. Scott, sounding puzzled.

"That sounds like . . . Mr. Burger!" said Henry.

"Does this dog have a tattoo?" asked Violet, pointing to the dog's inner thigh.

"Why, yes. I wrote it down on her forms when she was checked in." Dr. Scott paused to think.

"Do you know how to find out who she is registered to?" asked Henry.

"Yes, of course," said Dr. Scott. "There's a number you can call."

"Sunny is registered to Mrs. Annabel Teague," said Jessie.

Turning, Dr. Scott said, "I'm going to check this out right now. Wait here, please!"

A few minutes later the veterinarian came briskly back. "Sure enough — Annabel Teague is the owner," she said.

"It *is* Sunny! I knew it, I knew it!" Benny

jumped up and down with excitement.

"Good work, Benny," said Jessie. "I'm sorry I didn't believe you."

"That's okay. Watch believed me, didn't you Watch? Good boy!" Benny hugged the dog.

"We'd better call Caryn and tell her the good news," said Violet.

"Yes, and she can come pick up Sunny!" said Jessie.

"Wait a minute," said Henry. "Let *me* call Caryn. I have an idea. A way we could catch the person who did this!"

"What is it?" asked Jessie.

"Let me talk to Caryn about my idea," said Henry. "If she agrees, I'll tell you all about it."

And he hurried off to call Caryn with the good news about Sunny — and his mysterious idea.

CHAPTER 10

And the Winner Is . . .

At last it was evening, and the contest the Best of Show, the best dog at the First Annual Greenfield Dog Show, was about to begin. In their ringside seats, the Aldens and Mrs. Teague leaned forward eagerly.

One by one the seven dogs were led into the center of the arena. As each dog walked in, the crowd cheered wildly. Every dog was a champion, even if it didn't win Best of Show.

Lawrence Burger walked into the ring

with Plum at his side. He had a confident, superior little smile on his face. Beside him, Plum looked every inch a winner.

The Aldens applauded with the rest of the crowd, not for Lawrence Burger, but for his dog.

Mr. Burger took up his place in the ring and turned to face the center.

There was a pause. Then Caryn, dressed in a long glittery skirt and a silky blouse, led Sunny into the ring.

The crowd cheered. The Aldens cheered loudest of all.

Then Violet touched Jessie's arm to get her attention. "Look at Mr. Burger!"

Lawrence Burger wasn't cheering. His face was turning red. He looked like he was about to explode.

"It can't be," he cried. "That dog *can't* be here. I know because I left her at — "

Suddenly he stopped, his mouth open, his face even redder.

"What did you say?" asked the judge. She walked over and stood in front of Lawrence Burger.

"Nothing . . . I mean . . ."

The judge held up her hand. Several officials and other judges hurried into the ring. They took Caryn and Sunny, and Lawrence Burger and Plum off to one side while the crowd buzzed with astonished talk.

The Aldens quickly went to join Caryn and Sunny. Dr. Scott left her seat across the arena and came down into the ring, too.

"I would like an explanation of what is going on at *once*," said the judge sternly.

Lawrence Burger opened and closed his mouth like a fish gasping for air.

"We can explain," said Jessie, stepping forward.

"You? What do you know about this?" asked an official.

"A great deal," said Caryn. "They're the ones who found Sunny — and solved the mystery of why everything seemed to be going wrong at this dog show."

"Very well," said the judge. "Go ahead."

The Aldens took turns explaining all of the things that had gone wrong at the dog show. Then Dr. Scott identified Lawrence Burger as the man who had brought Sunny into her office to board her that morning, signing his name as Mr. Smith. When they had finished, the judge turned to face Lawrence Burger. "Did you do all those things?" she asked.

The proud, unpleasant look had left Lawrence Burger's face. Now he just looked miserable. "Yes," he confessed. "It was me. I shaved Curly so he wouldn't be able to compete for Best of Show. I knew that the dog favored to win the terrier group hated cats, so I — borrowed — that cat and turned it loose in the show. I even let out the air in the tires on Mrs. DeCicco's assistant's car. I hoped it would upset her and her dogs so much that they wouldn't do well. And I — borrowed — Sunny and took her to this veterinarian's office. I was going to go get her tomorrow morning and bring her back, honestly."

The judge shook her head. "This is bad, very bad." She and the other judges and officials stepped to one side and talked among themselves for a few minutes. Then the judge came back. "You are officially disqualified from this show. And you may be barred from showing dogs for a long time to come. You have disgraced the world of dog shows. And you have disgraced a fine dog. Your dog might well have won, fair and square. Now he may never get the chance to win again. You are dismissed."

His head hanging, Lawrence Burger walked miserably out of the ring. As they left, Plum licked his hand as if to try and comfort him. Mr. Burger looked down at Plum, stroked his head, then covered his eyes and hurried out of sight.

A few minutes later, the Reserve Champion was led into the arena to take Plum's place. The contest for Best in Show began.

It seemed to take the judge forever to look at each dog.

"I wish the judge would hurry up and decide," whispered Violet.

Mrs. Teague pressed her hand to her chest. "So do I!"

Henry leaned forward. "She *must* see that Caryn and Sunny are the best."

"Oh, I hope so!" said Jessie.

"Go, go, go, Sunny," said Benny.

At last the judge signaled for the seven dogs to circle the arena once more. And once again, the crowd cheered and cheered for the seven champions. Then the cheers rose to a thunder pitch as the judge pointed, 1,2,3,4 for the dogs that won first, second, third, and fourth.

"She won! She won!" cried Henry, jumping up.

"HOORAY FOR SUNNY!" shouted Benny.

All of the Aldens began to hug each other and Mrs. Teague, who was dabbing at her eyes with her sleeve. "Oh, I am so proud of Caryn and of Sunny," she kept saying. "So proud of them both!"

"They're real champions," Jessie said. "Even after everything that happened, they went out and won."

"Yes," agreed Mrs. Teague. "Oh, yes."

"Oh, good!" said Violet. "I was so excited that I almost didn't realize it, but Mrs. DeCicco's beagle Gloria came in second!"

"I'm so glad," said Jessie wholeheartedly.

"Let's go see everyone," said Benny, bouncing out of his seat.

"Okay, Benny," said Grandfather Alden. Together the Aldens and Mrs. Teague made their way through the excited crowd toward Sunny and Caryn.

"Congratulations!" called Violet as they passed Mrs. DeCicco, who was posing with Gloria for the photographers.

"Thank you!" answered Mrs. DeCicco, beaming. She kissed the top of Gloria's head and Gloria licked Mrs. DeCicco's face.

"Great shot," said one of the photographers, and everyone laughed. A moment later, they joined the Teagues and Sunny.

Just then, a familiar couple went by. "Come on, Zonker," said the polka-dot woman to the dalmatian at her side. "Time to go home."

The man beside her said, "You know, after this show, I think you're right. Maybe we all need a vacation."

The woman smiled.

"Oh, good," said Violet softly.

"Henry, Jessica, Violet, Benny — come

have your photograph taken with us. After all, if it hadn't been for you, Sunny wouldn't have been in the show at all!" Caryn said.

"Wait a minute!" cried Benny. "We *forgot*! We forgot the surprise!" He ran back to their seats.

"What surprise?" Caryn asked.

"You'll see," promised Henry as Benny came running back with the banner under his arm. Quickly, the Aldens unfurled the banner and held it up.

Caryn laughed with delight. "It's *wonderful*. Come on, let's all have our picture taken with it!"

As the Aldens joined the Teagues and Sunny, a young man came up to them. "It's a real scoop," he said. "What a story! How about an exclusive interview?"

"Well," said Jessie. Then she stopped. Her eyes widened. "I don't believe it!" she said. "What are *you* doing here?"

"I'm a reporter," said the man.

The Aldens all stared. It was the same man they had seen at the basset hound's cage, and lurking in the background when Curly had

been shaved, and near the entrance where the cat had first been seen at the show.

"A reporter," repeated Violet. "But what were you doing at the basset hound's cage? And when Curly got shaved — you were right there!"

"Yes," said Jessie. "And you were right there when the cat got in, too!"

The reporter shrugged. "That's what reporters do. We go where the action is! Besides, I wanted to be anonymous so I could get a real scoop. And I have!"

The Aldens burst out laughing at their mistake. "Great, great," said the reporter. He turned to the photographer. "Did you get that shot, Mac?"

"You were great, Caryn," said Henry.

Caryn gave Henry an excited little hug and he blushed as shyly as Violet. "Sunny was great," she said, "thanks to you and your brother and sisters."

"And Watch!" said Benny. He let go of his end of the banner, and flung his arms around Caryn and then around Sunny. "Watch is the one who really solved the mystery. He proved it was Sunny at Dr. Scott's. Watch is a champion, too."

"He certainly is," said Caryn. She smiled down at Benny. "Hooray for Watch!"

"Hooray for Sunny and for Watch!" cried Benny.

GERTRUDE CHANDLER WARNER discovered when she was teaching that many readers who like an exciting story could find no books that were both easy and fun to read. She decided to try to meet this need, and her first book, *The Boxcar Children*, quickly proved she had succeeded.

Miss Warner drew on her own experiences to write each mystery. As a child she spent hours watching trains go by on the tracks opposite her family home. She often dreamed about what it would be like to set up housekeeping in a caboose or freight car — the situation the Alden children find themselves in.

When Miss Warner received requests for more adventures involving Henry, Jessie, Violet, and Benny Alden, she began additional stories. In each, she chose a special setting and introduced unusual or eccentric characters who liked the unpredictable.

While the mystery element is central to each of Miss Warner's books, she never thought of them as strictly juvenile mysteries. She liked to stress the Aldens' independence and resourcefulness and their solid New England devotion to using up and making do. The Aldens go about most of their adventures with as little adult supervision as possible — something else that delights young readers.

Miss Warner lived in Putnam, Connecticut, until her death in 1979. During her lifetime, she received hundreds of letters from girls and boys telling her how much they liked her books.